THE
MOON
CAME
TOO

THE
MOON
CAME
TOO

by Nancy White Carlstrom

illustrated by Stella Ormai

Macmillan Publishing Company   New York
Collier Macmillan Publishers   London

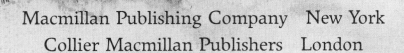

For Mom, Carolie,
and Allyson Grace
– N.W.C.

For Angelia Joy
– S.O.

Macmillan Publishing Company
866 Third Avenue, New York, NY 10022
Collier Macmillan Canada, Inc.
Printed and bound in Japan
First American Edition

10 9 8 7 6 5 4 3 2 1

The text of this book is set in 14 point Breughel.
The illustrations are rendered in ink and watercolor.

Library of Congress Cataloging-in-Publication Data
Carlstrom, Nancy White. The moon came too.
Summary: A young child excitedly plans all the essentials
she must take with her for a trip to Grandma's house.
[1. Stories in rhyme. 2. Grandmothers—Fiction]
I. Ormai, Stella, ill. II. Title.
PZ8.3.C1948Mo 1987 [E] 86-18046
ISBN 0-02-717380-1

Hooray hooray
We're going away
Going on a trip
To Grandma's house.

Going to the lake
What will I take
What will I take
To Grandma's house?

My fuzzy bear
And windup duck

My knotted rope
And yellow truck.

A bat and ball
And big bell that rings

Sam Cat, Ragdoll
And Rabbit, who sings.

A blue flashlight
Five books and a kite
Kangaroo Snuggle-de-loo

An owl that hoots
And a horn that toots
Maybe one puzzle will do.

Mama says *clothes*
Don't forget *clothes*
Better take *clothes*
To Grandma's house.

My overalls
With pockets of rocks

My boots and cape
And one pair of socks
That's enough!

But hats, hats
I'll need two or three

One for the barn
One for the tree
And one for the fishing
I'll do in the lake.

And oh that reminds me
I might as well take
My fishing pole
Some hooks and string
My box of stuff
And my good luck ring
That looks like a mouse.

Are there plenty of worms
At Grandma's house?

Get in the car
If you can fit
We're going now
Where will you sit?

There is certainly
Not much room
You brought everything
But the moon.

I talk to Owl
As we go along
Rabbit and Snuggle
Are singing a song
Singing a song
To Grandma's house.

I read some books
With my blue flashlight
Darker and darker
Hums the gray night
Humming along
To Grandma's house.

We close our eyes
Just for a moment
And then we're there
Before we know it
We're pulling up
To Grandma's house.

Grandma, Grandma
See what I brought

Rocks in my pocket
A rope in a knot
Books and a kite
And my good-luck-ring mouse
Grandma I hope
You have worms at your house.

My fishing stuff
Is right here with me
My cape and boots
And my hats all three.

Rabbit and Owl
And my windup duck
My bat and ball
And my yellow truck
I have my bear
And Snuggle-de-loo

Grandma look up
The moon came too.